ANNE - MAIL ORDER BRIDE

THE CHRISTMAS BRIDES OF JEFFERSON CITY

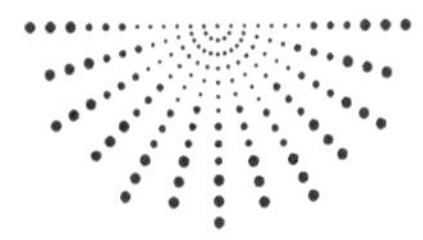

INDIANA WAKE

BELLE FIFFER

The Christmas Brides of Jefferson City

Everything was in bloom in Jefferson City at the beginning of summer but the Mayor had only one thing on his mind. He wanted to find wives for his sons by Christmas!

Mayor Arnold Foster is a dominant man that not many want to cross. When he demands that Pastor Thomas Brooks find Mail Order Brides for all *Six* of his sons the good pastor is reluctant. The Mayor will not be thwarted and resorts to threats. Pastor Brooks reluctantly agrees, knowing that he is the better person to take care of the women than whomever the mayor would get next.

Mayor Foster's sons are in no hurry to marry, in fact, they are totally against anything their father could suggest. Six strong and stubborn men will not be easy to persuade.

Pastor Brooks must rely on his faith and strength of character to find the perfect women for the Foster men. He is determined to find matches that will bring love and peace into all the lives of those involved.

Will Pastor Brooks succeed in bringing love to Jefferson City just in time for Christmas?

The books in this series each tell a complete story of one couple

The Christmas Brides of Jefferson City

Nicola

Amy

Polly

Shelley

Anne

Jacira

Tracy

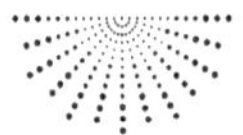

CHAPTER ONE

Doctor Ernest Foster sat back and began to tidy away his things.

"That's done. You don't need to be such a weakling next time, Chris."

"Weakling?" Chris scowled and gently prodded at his forehead, feeling the rough texture of the bandage under his hand. "How can I be a weakling when you're taking stitches out of my head? Stitches *you* put there last week?"

Ernest's mouth twitched in a slight smile, but he did not slow in what he was doing. "I was going to call you something else, but then I might get arrested for demeaning a lawman."

Chris's head was hurting too much for him to argue so he just grunted out his disapproval. Brothers, who'd have them? He could still feel the stitches in his head. At least the wound had virtually healed so the stitches weren't needed anymore. If only the same could be said about the stitches in his stomach. They were keeping his stomach sewn up and his insides where they should be. Chris could feel them tugging at his body.

Though he guessed he was mainly mad at himself. He'd never let anyone get the drop on him before. Chris considered himself young and strong. A criminal might have sucker-punched him a few times, but he had never come out worse before. Yet, in the space of ten days, one man had stabbed him to the point he almost died and then another smashed him over the head with a bottle, splitting his head open and making him lose his senses for some time. Ernest had said Chris was lucky both times, and Chris was counting his blessings. He didn't want to lose all his lives so quickly.

Luckily, his head was better, and his stomach would mend. Eventually. Providing Chris didn't end up getting beaten up anytime soon. Considering how disruptive Christmas seemed to be with everyone this year, that was going to be interesting.

Ernest turned to the woman across the room from him.

"Jacira, could you sort these out for me, please? I'll just finish up with Sheriff Foster."

"All right, Doctor Foster."

The beautiful Indian woman crossed the room and took the tray from Ernest, Chris watching as a look passed between the two of them. He had to fight back a smile. For someone who said he wouldn't be losing his heart to anyone, Ernest had pretty much handed his over, tied up with a pretty bow, to Jacira, the healer.

Jacira moved away and Ernest turned to Chris, rubbing a hand over his beard with a sigh. "You need to rest, Chris."

"I'm fine. You've just taken the stitches out."

"Out of your head. Not the wound in your stomach." Ernest gestured at Chris' belly. "That's still not good and you don't want to be pulling those stitches or aggravating the wound."

Chris knew that much. He felt like the knife was still stuck in him when he moved too much. Everything had to be done a little gingerly, and the attack from a man who had killed his wife hadn't helped. Chris was still annoyed that the man had got the jump on him. That never happened.

Don't lie. It happens all the time. You've just never been on the back foot like this before.

Chris sighed and pressed his fingers to his temples. Either Ernest had put the bandage on his head a little too tight, or he was going to suffer a very bad headache.

"I'm not woozy or sick. I'm just dealing with the sensation of being hit over the head with a glass bottle. And I'm just going to stick to the office for now while my deputies go out and do the physical stuff. I'm not going after criminals or dealing with bar brawls."

"You'd better not." Ernest snorted. "Doctor's orders say you shouldn't until I give the all-clear."

"And when will that be?"

"When I decide you're fit." Ernest turned to his desk

and picked up a pen. "Otherwise, I'm tying you down to the bed with your own handcuffs."

Chris heard a giggle and glanced over at Jacira. She was cleaning and tidying away what Ernest had been using. There was a twinkle in her eye when she looked at Chris.

"He will do that as well," she said with a beautiful smile; despite the burn scar on her face she was a very attractive woman.

"I know." Chris glared at his brother. "But just because I'm the youngest doesn't mean I get to be bossed around. I am the sheriff, after all."

"And you're the youngest to hold the sheriff's position and the youngest to hold the position for two terms, I know." Ernest rolled his eyes. "You say that a lot, Chris. And while I'm glad you're breaking traditions and all that, it doesn't mean you're above the town's doctor, who happens to be your big brother."

Chris huffed. "You wouldn't be talking to me like that if you needed something from me. Like me shifting a few patients who refuse to leave."

Ernest sighed. "You act like a child at times, Chris. Especially now. No wonder, seeing as you were Mother's favorite."

"I was not Mother's favorite." Chris protested. "We just got along the best, all right. There was no favoritism. Father always wanted to be her favorite."

"And look where it got him." Ernest snorted. "Six children who want nothing to do with him."

Chris had often wondered why Arnold Foster would do that to himself. But from a young age, he had noticed that his father was a controlling man. He loved to be in charge and make sure everyone knew it. He had attempted to play each son off against each other, especially the twins, Ernest and Matthew. That had been interesting, seeing as Ernest and Matthew were the closest of the six of them. A bond they shared was not going to be broken by a father who wanted to treat everyone like puppets. Chris had no idea how their mother had dealt with this all her life, but it wasn't his place to ask. She had done things her way and it worked.

Losing her had been really difficult to handle. The only thing worse than that was when Olivia didn't turn up for his wedding. Chris still remembered the looks of pity from the guests, especially from his father when he wasn't full of rage. It was the one time Chris had wanted his father to be there for him, to be a parent. But instead, he had to make it about himself. Only a day later, he was forcing Pastor Thomas Brooks to bring in brides for all of his sons. He didn't care about them at all.

Chris would be happy not having to speak to the man again, but in his position, he had to be in frequent contact with Foster. As the mayor, he was heavily involved in everything. At least he wasn't in charge of who was selected for sheriff; otherwise, Chris would have been refused any type of law job at all. Foster hated the fact that another of their brothers, Morgan, was a US Marshal, and he was only just coming to terms with his youngest son being the sheriff. Successful, yes, but the job description wasn't what he wanted. It didn't have the prestige that the mayor wanted.

It didn't matter to the brothers, the man could get lost as far as Chris was concerned. Ernest had also come to this decision long ago.

"If you hate Father so much, why haven't you moved away?" Ernest asked.

"Why haven't you?" Chris sighed.

"I asked first."

"Because I'm the sheriff in a position I was voted in for by the townspeople. I can't exactly move, not until my term is up and if I'm not re-elected... who knows. You, on the other hand, can. Everyone else can, even Adam and Matt. My skills and job title aren't exactly transferable."

"They can be if you want them to be," Jacira pointed out. "You could even go into work with Morgan."

Chris snorted. "We'd end up hunting each other by the end of the week."

Jacira shook her head. "No, you wouldn't."

"Yes, they would," Ernest countered. "We would all be hunting Chris at the end of the week. He's the thick-headed idiot who will go walking into knives and glass bottles."

"Not fair!" Chris protested.

"Well, you are thick-headed." Ernest sat back in his

chair and folded his arms. "I want you, Sheriff Foster, to go straight home and rest. No arguments. Make sure Mrs. Bracey knows to keep an eye on you. She or one of us can do your errands and all that until I say you can do them for yourself."

Chris could feel his face getting warm. Why did he have to mention Anne Bracey? It was like Ernest seemed to know that any sniff of the woman and Chris would end up reacting in some way. Chris hated it when he did that. His brother was good at goading him, and Chris wished he wasn't the sheriff at times. He really wanted to throttle the good doctor and then he would have to throw himself in jail. He guessed it wasn't worth it.

Because Ernest, just like all of his brothers, knew that the lovely young widow had an effect on Chris. It was something Chris hated to be reminded about. He had vowed, just like his brothers, to not get involved romantically with any of the women his father had brought here. Matt, James, Morgan, and Adam had failed in that vow and were all engaged to be married. It was just Chris and Ernest now, and Chris knew that Ernest had a perfectly solid excuse for not falling for any of the young ladies... Jacira.

So that just left him. And Chris had told himself he would not go through it again. Especially not at Christmas. Not after last time.

Try telling yourself that and see if you can sound more convincing.

"I'm not asking Anne to look after me."

"Why not? She's done plenty for you over the last couple of weeks." Ernest chuckled. "I seem to remember she looked after you when you got ridiculously drunk on your birthday back in August. Tucked you in like a baby."

Chris growled. "You know why I drank so much on that day, Ernest."

"I do know, and I'm also trying to say that Anne Bracey can easily take care of you if you so much as said a word about it. When she's loyal, she's loyal."

That was something. But Chris didn't want a woman in his life. Did he?

Again, tell yourself that when you don't sound like you're lying to yourself. You've got it bad for Anne Bracey and you're too cowardly to admit it.

"She's got a child, Ernest. She's not going to drop everything for me when she's got a four-year-old to look after. And I'm not going to demand anything of her."

"From what I hear, she's more than happy to help."

Chris groaned. The man just would not let up. "How are you Matt's twin? He wouldn't be bugging me like this."

Ernest laughed and turned back to his desk. "Get out of here, Chris. And I mean it when I say rest. You don't want me to double up the stitches, do you?"

Chris decided against giving him a rude gesture and left his brother's office. The man was insufferable, and Chris was surprised that he was so popular if that was what he considered a bedside manner. Maybe he was different with his own family.

Then again, considering who their father was, it was hardly a surprise that the bedside manner was non-existent. Although the ladies certainly didn't seem to mind. They came out in droves with minor ailments just to be in Ernest's company. Chris found it laughable. Matthew certainly teased his twin about it, but Ernest was good at ignoring it all.

Great doctor, lousy manners.

Jacira followed Chris out into the waiting room, giving him a smile as she moved ahead of him.

"Ignore him. He's being a pain right now."

"How's that different than normal?"

"I think something's catching in this town with all this love in the air with your brothers." Jacira's eyes twinkled as she looked at him. "Either that or he loves teasing you."

"He loves to tease me all the time," Chris grunted. "And I'm not getting married again. Not after what happened."

"I know." Jacira squeezed his arm. "But don't discard it completely. One day, the woman you do want to marry will come along and you'll do anything not to let her go."

That was Jacira all over. Such a kind heart. Even after everything she had gone through, she was the sweetest person Chris had ever met. It was no wonder Ernest was in love with her. Chris kissed her scarred cheek.

"I hope my brother does the same thing with you one day. Otherwise, he's a fool."

"Don't talk like that, Chris." Jacira's smile faded. "I'm afraid it's not going to happen."

"Will it not?" Chris put on his Stetson and gave her a nod. "Goodnight, Jacira."

He stepped out into the cool evening. The light had started to fade already, and the shadows were getting longer. It wasn't as cold here as it was further west, but the nights were starting to have a distinct chill to the air. Just like every other Christmas.

Chris started walking in the direction of his home, still thinking about his brother and Jacira. It was a shame that Ernest was focused on his decision that he wasn't going to get married. Because he and Jacira would be perfect. He didn't care what people thought, and it was clear to anyone that his feelings for her were reciprocated. It was a wonder Ernest hadn't asked Jacira to marry him a long time ago. Maybe he would realize one day that he needed to step up and take the plunge. Not even a patient woman like Jacira would wait around forever.

Shoving his hands into his pockets, Chris tried not to

focus on the ache in his stomach. It wasn't just from the stitches tugging at his wounds. That was irritating, but it wasn't what was bothering him.

He hated Christmas. Had done since he was a child. But now it was pretty much ruined after last year. Olivia had wanted a Christmas wedding, saying that it was incredibly romantic. Chris hadn't wanted to do that, but he wasn't about to deny his future wife what she wanted, so he had agreed. Only to be waiting at the altar while Olivia ran off with her childhood sweetheart, who had come back into her life a few weeks before.

Chris should have been more suspicious. Maybe in his gut, he had thought that she and this former flame were over and they were going to behave like regular adults. But that hadn't happened. Olivia had decided running off on her wedding day to the man she had loved as a girl was the best thing to do, ignoring all the wedding preparations her parents had paid for and set up for their only daughter to have the perfect wedding. They had been just as embarrassed as Chris.

As far as he knew, neither of Olivia's parents spoke to her anymore. If she was even in contact with them. Olivia's brother certainly hadn't forgiven his sister for what she did. Chris was... hurt so much by it that... he was just done. Olivia had just proved to him that Christmas was the worst possible day for him.

That letter she had left, conveniently put on his kitchen table while Chris was at the church waiting for her, had been soul-destroying. Chris had already had his heart ripped out of him, and then she said all those things about not loving him anymore and how she never truly loved him. She tried to make it all Chris's fault, and for a while, Chris had believed it was his fault. He had not been attentive enough? Maybe he worked too hard? Had he been the reason everything went wrong? But the more he picked apart everything, the more he knew that this was nothing to do with him and everything to do with Olivia being an entitled young lady who didn't care who she hurt as long as she got what she wanted.

Chris had thrown the letter into the fire. And wished he could throw Olivia there as well. But she wasn't here. If she did turn up in Jefferson City again, Chris knew he would do everything to drive her out. His brothers certainly would. Nobody humiliated and hurt their baby brother.

Baby brother. Chris hadn't been that in a long time. But compared to everyone else, he was the baby of the family. Their protective streak over him was rather amusing, seeing as he was the one with the authority in town.

What were his brothers going to do for Christmas? Were they going to have those weddings that their father kept talking about? He was so determined to have all of his sons married on Christmas Day. Chris didn't understand the obsession, but that wasn't happening to him. If he got married, ever, it wasn't going to be on that day. Not even if a gun was put to his head.

There were too many bad memories already. A wedding wasn't going to cancel all of them out.

"Mama!"

Chris slowed when he heard the cry. It was one of a child. Then he heard another one. A woman. She was shouting, the little girl screaming. Chris's heart sank when he realized who it was.

It was coming from the alley ahead of him. Fumbling for his pistol, Chris ran, taking a sharp right turn into the alley. A woman was fighting with someone dressed all in black, her hair loose and wrapped in the man's fist. He was a lot taller than her, his face hidden by shadows. A little girl stood nearby, huddled against the wall as she wailed.

Anne and Tamsin.

Chris felt the rage. Attacking a woman was one thing, but when there was a child involved? That was something else. He fired once, aiming at a point just above the attacker's head.

"Sheriff! Let her go!"

He fired again, this time a little lower. The man snarled and threw Anne aside. She hit the wall and went down before laying still. Then her attacker ran, charging back down the alley. Chris fired again, but it was wide and ricocheted off the brick. Moments later, the man was gone around the corner. Chris would have taken off after him, but he didn't think his stitches would hold if he ran. And the sight of the little girl sobbing over her mother's limp body was enough for him to stay.

Holstering his weapon, Chris approached the girl. "Tamsin?"

Tamsin looked up, her eyes shining with tears. Then she ran at Chris so hard she almost knocked him over, wrapping her arms around his waist.

"Uncle Chris!"

"It's me, sweetie." Chris bit back the pain as she inadvertently hit his stomach. He stroked her hair, his heart cracking as he felt her shaking like a leaf. "What happened?"

"We were going home, and he came out behind her and he grabbed me and Mama got between us and I..."

"Whoa, whoa, slow down." Chris eased back a little and knelt, cupping the little girl's head. "Look at me, Tamsin. Are you all right?"

"I think so." Tamsin's voice was tiny, almost audible now. Tears streaked her cheeks. "Mama didn't let him hurt me. I think he knew us."

"Why do you say that?"

"Because he called her Annie. Mama hates it when she's called Annie. Uncle Yves and Grandmother and Grandfather called her that because they knew she hated it."

Even Chris knew it. He had attempted to call her that once, just to lighten the mood, and it had just made Anne really angry. Chris had backed off on that afterward. He knew when he had to step back. Anne had made that really clear.

Did that mean someone from her family had come after her?

Shifting around the little girl, Chris crawled over to Anne. She was stirring, shifting a little in the dirt. Her blonde hair had been pulled out of its carefully pinned position, leaving it in a tangled mess. The pins were still in her strands. Chris knelt beside her, stroking her hair out of her face.

"Anne? Anne, can you hear me?"

Anne moaned, but she didn't open her eyes. Chris looked up at Tamsin, who was watching him and making little whimpers.

"Go and find Doctor Foster. He's still in the surgery. If you can't find him, find Jacira. Tell them I'm bringing a patient in."

Tamsin nodded and then ran off. Chris had no doubt that the four-year-old would find Ernest. The first person she ran to after Chris was always Ernest. Chris had never quite figured out why, but in this instance he was glad.

There was a moan from Anne, and Chris saw her eyes flutter open. She still looked dazed, a bruise was coming up under her eye. Her gaze landed on him, but she didn't seem to be comprehending that he was there.

"Sheriff?" She sounded as dazed as she looked. "Is... what...?"

"Don't talk. Just keep yourself awake." Chris eased his arms under her and lifted her into his arms. "I've got you. Let's get you to the doctor."

"He..." Anne barely reacted as Chris rose to his feet. "He was going..."

Chris pressed a kiss to her forehead before he hurried out of the alley.

"I know, honey. I know."

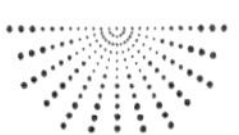

$\mathcal{E}$rnest stepped back and gave Anne a gentle smile.

"You're going to have a sore head, but you're going to be fine. Just cuts and bruises. It could have been a lot worse."

Anne snorted. "I've had worse."

Ernest barely batted an eyelid. After the bruises he had seen on her when Anne first arrived, it didn't take a blind man to know that Anne had escaped from a bad situation. Ernest had commented that it was a wonder Anne wasn't dead already.

Anne had wondered that herself. With her head

feeling like it was about to split open, she was having moments when she wished that had happened. But then she was reminded of her daughter, and that made her grit her teeth. She hated pain, but she hated leaving Tamsin alone. She would never do that to her child.

"Where's Tamsin?" Anne glanced towards the door. "Is she still with Jacira?"

"She is, and Jacira said that she's fine but shaken." Ernest gave her a gentle smile. "She'll stay with her until you've finished here."

"Have you finished with me?"

"I have." Ernest paused and glanced over his shoulder. "But he hasn't."

Anne didn't need to look into the corner. She had felt Chris's eyes on her the whole time she was been checked over by the doctor. Chris had carried her into the surgery, refusing to leave her as she came around. He still refused to budge from the room, and Anne was conflicted between being glad he was there and wishing he would go. She was a mix of emotions right now. Chris had had to see that, see her in such a state after Anne had tried so hard to be strong. It was something she didn't want to happen again.

But at least it had been Chris. And Anne was glad he had been close by. If Yves had dragged her away at that point...

Anne shook herself. She wasn't going to think about that. Not now. She didn't get taken away. Chris had saved her. He had looked after her.

He had kissed her. Anne could still feel the press of his lips on her forehead. It certainly made her feel warm. How many times over the last six months had she wished that Chris would kiss her? This was not quite the kiss that she wanted, but she would take what she could.

It was just typical of her. She ran away from her deceased husband's family, only to fall in love with someone who was dead set against having any woman in his life. Anne just couldn't pick men well. Francois had come with a bad family, and Chris just came with bad experiences.

Anne understood that, far too well.

"I'm going to check on Tamsin and Jacira." Ernest glanced at Chris. "I'll give you a few minutes."

"Right."

Ernest sighed and left the room. Anne looked at Chris. He was leaning against the wall with his arms folded and a scowl on his handsome face. He had barely moved since putting Anne on the couch in his brother's office, giving them as much distance as possible without leaving the room. Even Anne could feel the distance. She wanted to have his arms around her again, only this time with her fully conscious.

For the first time in her life, Anne wanted to be selfish.

Not now. You have to focus on the fact that Yves is here. And if he's here, you and Tamsin need to run.

Chris needs to know about this.

Does he?

Old instincts came back, and Anne found herself backing away from wanting help. She didn't want anyone to know. She looked away.

"I don't want to press charges."

"Why would you not?"

Anne winced. Chris sounded outraged at that. Anne couldn't blame him for that, but she couldn't get out of bad habits.

"Because…" She looked at the floor. "It doesn't matter."

There was silence. Then gentle footsteps. Anne saw Chris's boots appear before her, and he waited. She didn't dare look up even as her heart started picking up speed as she stared at the dusty boots. Just the mere presence of this man had Anne feeling like a young girl again. She was a widow and a mother. She shouldn't be this shy around a man.

Should she?

"Anne."

Anne refused to look up. It was only when Chris knelt down and his fingers brushed under her chin and urged her to look up that she gave in. He was standing close to her, almost a little too close, his face inches from hers. Anne's heart was racing so fast it was a wonder she didn't pass out.

"Anne," Chris' fingers stroked her jaw, running over her cheek, "you were attacked. You could've been killed. Then Tamsin would be alone. Do you want that?"

"Don't try and guilt me into telling you, Sheriff." Anne jerked her head away. "Tamsin would have been fine. Better off with my friends than..."

"Than whom? The man who attacked you?" Chris's eyes narrowed. "Tamsin said he said your name. Annie. A name I know you hate."

Oh, my Lord. Anne had almost forgotten about that. Tamsin had heard that? She swallowed.

"Tamsin was mistaken. That didn't happen."

Chris shook his head.

"Your daughter is very clever. She may be four years old, but that girl is sharp. Don't insult your child's intelligence. It doesn't become you."

It would just take a conversation with Tamsin and then it would all come out. Anne knew that word would get around town and then everyone in Jefferson City would know about what happened to her. She trusted Chris to keep it quiet, but there were less scrupulous people around. And Tamsin had a habit of telling her life story if you gave her half a chance. Anne swallowed, still unable to look at Chris.

"I don't want to talk about it."

Chris sighed and ran his hand through his dark hair. Was he already going silver at the temples? He was going to look like Matthew the older he got. Anne had a soft spot for Matthew, whose little girl was a real sweetheart. She would not mind if Chris's hair went silver.

"You're going to have to talk about it at some point, Anne. Because whoever attacked you knows you. And they want to hurt you and maybe even your daughter too."

Anne swallowed, no, not that, but they wouldn't. "It's nothing I can't handle."

"Considering how I found you, I doubt it."

Anne glared at him. "You don't know a thing about me, Chris. I'm more than capable."

Chris's eyes flashed. Was it because she had argued back? Or was it because she called him Chris? That didn't happen often, Anne trying to maintain formalities. If she slipped, then she would begin to relax. Anne couldn't do that. Not just yet.

"I don't doubt that you're capable, Anne, but the fact that I don't know a thing about you is rubbish." He pressed his hands on either side of her, effectively pinning her in. He had never been this close to her before, and she felt a delightful shiver up her spine with his face inches from hers.

"You keep things to yourself, but I know that you would do anything for Tamsin. Even if it means getting hurt in the process. The fear I see in your eyes right now? It's not fear for your safety. It's fear that Tamsin's not going to have someone to protect her."

"Stop it, Chris."

"You want me to stop? You'd better tell me what's going on." Chris shook his head. "I can't help you if you don't help me."

And Anne wanted him to help. Deep down, she wanted Chris there. But pride got in the way. And the fear stopped her from saying anything. Which was ridiculous, because she couldn't be touched now.

Anne had got away, and her former family didn't know where she was. She had nothing to fear now. Only, she was always scared that one day they would turn up and demand that she returned. That nobody would stand up for her.

She had wanted to tell Chris over the last six months. Anne had come to trust the young sheriff. He was like his brothers, tall, dark, and irrepressible, but he had a big heart. The Foster brothers would give you the shirt off their backs if you asked. Anne could be sure that Chris would want to help, but her in-laws were nasty people. People with their fingers in a lot of pies. They could make her look like the manic woman who ran away because she was unstable.

Anne was not going back, and it was best that Chris didn't know about her past. She fixed him with a cool stare, wishing that he wasn't so close.

"I'm not about to do that. This is my problem. A problem I had left behind."

"Well, it's followed you here." Chris snorted. "And you can't handle it alone."

"Try me."

But Chris shook his head. He didn't look angry. Frustrated, yes, but not angry. And worried? Worried about her? Surely, not.

"No, I won't. Because you'll tell me eventually."

"You think I will?"

"I know you will."

Did he think he knew her? The two of them could spend hours talking about anything and everything, and Anne managed to keep most of her past to herself. It was off-limits, as far as she was concerned. If she could keep that from Chris for six months, she could do it a little longer.

Why don't you swallow your pride and actually tell him? He wants to help.

If I tell him, he'll end up getting hurt. I know he will.

Chris was still close, his eyes searching her face. Anne wondered how he would react if she leaned forward, just a little bit... so that their lips touched...

No, that was not happening. Anne took a deep breath and squared her shoulders.

"I want to see my daughter, Sheriff. Then we'll head

back to the boarding house. I think I need to get some sleep.”

For a moment, she thought Chris was not going to let her. But he eventually moved away and slowly rose to his feet with a wince, pressing a hand to his stomach.

“Do you want an escort?”

“I’ll ask Jacira to escort me.” Anne stood up, stepping away from him. “Nobody messes with her.”

“At least let me make sure you get inside without being accosted again.”

He was persistent, Anne had to give him that much. She had to admire that about him. Just like the rest of his brothers, Chris would not let anything go. It was no wonder he was the sheriff at such a young age with no help from his father. Chris made his way on his own, and he was good at it.

Anne just wished he wouldn’t be persistent with her.

“You’ll hear it from Jacira.” She held up a hand as Chris started to protest. “Please, Chris, just... I just want to go home.”

Home. The boarding house. It wasn't exactly a home, but Anne was glad that Maria Brooks let her stay there, paying for her and Tamsin's room by doing extra chores and helping out. Maria had offered to pay Anne but Anne had eventually agreed, feeling awful about saying Maria could pay. Anne had been told by her in-laws that she should never ask for money or it would be seen as begging. She had a little money of her own, and she could go without food for a while. It was just Tamsin she needed to feed. It was no wonder she had lost so much weight, but Anne refused to rely on other people except herself.

Chris knew that. And he was staring at her like she had gone mad. But he sighed heavily and looked away.

"All right. But you and I do need to talk."

Talk. Anne knew what about, and that sent her into a panic.

"Not if I don't have to." She hurried to the door. "Goodnight, Sheriff Foster."

Her husband's family had messed her up more than she realized, and six months on, it was difficult to get used to a different pace of life where people were actually decent to her. Anne didn't know how to cope with it on most days. And she didn't know how to deal with Chris Foster.

Falling in love hadn't been on her list of priorities, they had just been to get away from the hell she was stuck in. Anne never expected to fall for the sheriff.

He's going to know sooner or later. And it's better that it's sooner and from you.

I know. But not now.

Maybe later. Anne didn't know. But as she collected Tamsin and left the surgery with Jacira, Anne knew it would have to be sooner than she was prepared for.

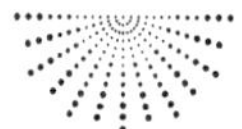

CHAPTER THREE

"Sheriff Foster?"

Chris barely looked up as he scribbled in his notebook as one of his deputies put his head around the door.

"What?"

"Mrs. Bracey's here. She said she wanted to speak to you."

That had Chris sitting up. Anne was here? She had left the night before barely able to look him in the eye. Chris had had a sleepless night trying to figure out what was going on with her. There were days when she would be warm and happy, that smile of hers making his heart swell, and then there were days when she was withdrawn and wouldn't see anyone. Chris had wanted to figure out what was happening, but he didn't want to be seen as chasing her. The fact was that Anne had been slightly skittish of him when they first met, it suggested that she wasn't comfortable with the law.

Chris knew he should have left her alone. If she didn't like the law and he wasn't looking for a wife - he knew exactly who had brought her to town - why was he seeking her out to be in her company? That didn't make sense. Chris had vowed that he would never let a woman get under his skin again and yet...

Anne had gotten under his skin, and she wasn't moving. The fact she had been losing weight worried Chris. She was going to be skin and bones if she carried on like that. Chris didn't want to see her collapse because she was giving everything to her sweet little girl and not herself.

It was strange that a woman could talk to him so much over recent months, and yet barely say anything about herself. Chris hadn't pushed, thinking he could gain her trust over time. Having Anne around, cleaning his house and looking after him when he was trying to recover at home after Dominic Growcott stabbed him, made him feel better. He was happier than he had been in a while, just by having her around. Even Tamsin made him feel good.

Who knew a child could help mend a broken heart?

Would you stop thinking about what Anne's done for you? She's outside and wants to talk to you. This is about her.

Chris shook himself, aware that his deputy was looking at him oddly. Clearing his throat, Chris got to his feet.

"Show her in."

The young man disappeared, and then the door opened wider to allow Anne inside. Chris took a moment to look her over. He liked looking at her. She looked petite, blonde, and delicate, but the woman was stronger than she made herself out to be. And the lioness that came out of her when Tamsin was threatened was startling. She was not like Olivia at all. Was probably as opposite as you could get.

No. No thoughts of Olivia. Get rid of her.

"Sheriff."

Anne folded her hands in front of her and watched him with her head held high. Even then, she was wavering a little. Chris wanted to reach out and touch her, but he was sure Anne would flinch away from him.

"Anne."

They stared at each other. Then Anne swallowed and gestured to a chair.

"Do you mind if I sit down?"

"No. No, of course not."

Anne sat down, smoothing her skirts down before folding her hands in her lap. Chris came around to her side and leaned against the desk.

"Where's Tamsin?"

"Tracy's looking after her for the day. I..." Anne licked her lips. "I wanted to speak to you in private."

"All right."

Chris waited. He wasn't about to push her. From the way she was trembling, this was something Anne was struggling with. If he pushed her too much, she was going to run. Chris didn't want that.

Anne took a deep breath and let it out slowly.

"Realize that this is very difficult for me. It's been... it's been five years and I'm still struggling a lot with it now. I know it's wrong, but... when it's ingrained into you..."

"Slow down, Anne." Chris held up a hand. "Start from the beginning. Help me understand."

"All right." Anne closed her eyes briefly. Then she opened them and looked up with her blue-gray eyes clear. Though she looked perfectly composed, Chris could see the nerves in the slight shake of her hands in her lap. "I was very rude to you last night. And I'm sorry. I don't like being rude, but I... I was scared."

"I got that bit. And I don't blame you for that."

From the flicker in her eyes, Anne thought Chris was going to berate her for her actions. Her shoulders slumped.

"You're too kind to me, Sheriff Foster."

That was not the reaction he expected. Chris frowned. "You think you don't deserve kindness?"

"No. Because..." Anne took a deep breath. "My family - my husband's family, rather - said that I didn't deserve anything nice. They had no idea why my husband even married me. Francois... he loved me. Did anything for me, even standing up to his family when they were horrible. So, they got to me when he wasn't around. I was sixteen when we married, and I had lost my parents a few months before, so they beat out whatever confidence I had. They made me... well, someone I didn't like."

Chris listened to this with a sinking feeling. He had suspected Anne had run away from abuse, but never anything like this. It would explain why she had been so nervous around him when they literally ran into each other. People suffering from abuse were scared into silence and wouldn't go to the law, mostly because the law wouldn't help them.

If Chris saw any abuse, he was first in line to defend the person, and he didn't care who knew it.

"Were they violent to you?"

"The lot of them were brawlers," Anne said bitterly.

"They couldn't handle their drink and always got violent when they even had a sip of whisky. I don't like to drink, and neither did Francois. Especially once we knew I was pregnant; he didn't want that around our child. But according to his parents and his brothers, I'm the one who corrupted him by keeping him sober." Anne's hands tightened in her lap. "I'm still trying to figure out the logic in that. Once Tamsin was born, Francois made sure that I was never left alone with them, and Tamsin was never allowed out of my sight. And yet I was the controlling one. Francois knew they could turn their violence onto Tamsin, and he didn't want to let her suffer it."

Then Francois had died. Chris remembered Anne telling him. A wave of influenza had hit the town they lived in and Francois was one of the many victims. Anne had been left with a young child and the only people in her life were her mean in-laws.

"They laid their hands on you?"

"They tried. But after Francois died, I always had a friend with me." Anne's mouth twitched in a slight smile. "Tracy stayed with me. She was a neighbor and always helped out when Francois was at work.

We became good friends and she and Polly always stood up for me. My in-laws didn't like that. They hated me, but they refused to let me go."

"I know a few people like that," Chris muttered.

Anne bit her lip.

"Then Francois's brother, Yves, started trying to come over. He... he said that now Francois was dead, he was next in line to marry me. Like I was to be passed around the brothers like a trophy. I hate Yves with a passion, and he thought he had priority over who I was to marry next?"

Chris stared. He had thought he had heard it all before.

"He can't do that if you're mourning, can he?"

"He could try. I would've said no the whole way through. Tracy told me a forced marriage is no marriage, especially when I'm constantly saying no." Anne scowled. "I told him, no, but he wouldn't listen. He set everything up at the church without my consent. I found out the night before when my mother-in-law turned up and said she was staying to get me ready. Tracy and Polly managed to get her out and arranged for me to leave. They were due to leave for here, anyway, and said I should come along with them. Nobody would know where I had gone."

"So, they brought you here to be a bride for someone else?"

Anne winced.

"Tracy said I didn't have to if I didn't want it, but the thought of getting away was too good to pass up. And I've not done too badly," she added with a gesture at her surroundings. "I like it here. People are really nice, and Tamsin's thriving with lots of friends."

Chris didn't think Anne was doing well, considering she looked like she was about to collapse. He knew that she went without at times so Tamsin could eat and she refused help. The guilt was still there from the family she married into, the words they threw at her still apparent. She didn't think she deserved anything and focused on Tamsin and other people.

Like Chris. Chris couldn't remember Anne eating while he was recovering at home, Anne always claimed that she was going to eat later. He didn't believe that now, and it pained him to see her suffering like this.

"I take it you're not interested in marriage, then."

Why did he even say that? He shouldn't care about that, surely?

Anne blinked, but she answered. "If it arises for me, I'll consider it. But I won't get married at Christmas. Not when..." Her voice wavered. "Francois died on Christmas morning."

"Oh." Chris cleared his throat. "I'm sorry."

Suddenly, his experience of being left at the altar felt insignificant. Anne had lost someone she had loved, someone who had married her regardless of everything.

"It's not just you with bad Christmas memories, you know, Sheriff," Anne said quietly. "I understand completely. And I want to have Tamsin experience a good Christmas. I want her to make new memories. There's nothing wrong with making new memories, is there?"

"Nothing at all," Chris murmured.

She was right. Holding onto bad memories was not going to help anyone. Making new memories for the same day, however… there shouldn't be a problem with that, should there?

Anne had bowed her head, and her shoulders were shaking. Chris's chest tightened. He leaned over and gently urged her to stand up. Anne obliged, much to his surprise, and leaned into him as he wrapped his arms around her.

"It's all right." Chris stroked her hair. She had left it in a loose braid, and her hair was so soft under his hand. "It's going to be all right."

Anne sniffed and rested her head on his shoulder. Her arms slipped around him, resting on his waist. It was a little uncomfortable on Chris' stomach, but he wasn't letting this go. He had Anne in his arms, and now he felt like he was safe. The past year he had been floundering, trying to figure out what was going to happen to him. Chris had felt numb for months after Olivia walked out on him. He didn't think he could pick himself up.

But Anne changed that. She grounded him, made him feel comfortable again. When she allowed physical contact, a touch or a hug, it was like everything settled down. Chris knew he shouldn't put things on someone else's shoulders, but it made him feel better knowing that he wasn't completely cold.

And he didn't want to let Anne go. So he rested his chin on her head and held her close. They didn't talk for a while, Chris simply letting Anne sniff and sob in his arms. He didn't think there was anything he could say right now, especially after what Anne had told him. But he knew he would do anything to make her smile again. A smile that made her sparkle.

You really do have it bad for her. And you ignored it for so long.

Because I'm a fool.

The sudden bang of a door and loud footsteps sounded outside before a deep voice reached their ears. Chris caught the name 'Annie', and then he felt Anne stiffen in his arms.

"Anne?" He eased her back, noticing that she had gone very pale. "What is it?"

"That's Yves." Anne's voice was barely above a whisper. "He's found me."

Chris could see she was about to collapse. He eased her down into her chair.

"Stay here. I don't want you stepping foot outside of this room until he's gone. I'll make him leave."

"What?" Anne stared at him. "But you're hurt. You can't face him down."

"I'm tougher than you think." Chris kissed her forehead. "I'll be fine. Just stay here and stay quiet. I won't let him back here."

If that man tried to touch her... Chris gritted his teeth as a wave of anger washed over him.

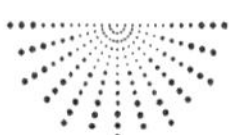

hris did his best to compose himself as he left his office, closing the door behind him. His brothers did tend to say he was emotional and it showed in his face. He didn't want to lose his temper with the man demanding Anne be returned to him. Chris could hear him berating Deputy Terence Bignall, saying that he was taking his bride back and he had better get the sheriff to help him.

At least Terence was discreet. Chris had a policy with everyone in town that if someone who wasn't from Jefferson City came to town demanding to see someone, they were not to say anything and simply direct them to Chris. He could deal with them. Mostly because there were plenty of people trying to find someone who had run away in the first place and were refusing to go back. Chris wanted to protect the townspeople as much as he could.

That included Anne. Especially Anne.

Putting his Stetson on and squaring his shoulders, Chris headed out into the lobby. Terence was standing behind his desk with a large, pot-bellied man in his late twenties leaning on the desk with one hand while the other one shook in Terence's face. Chris took one look at him and his gut knew that this was the man who had tried to attack Anne the night before. Right down to the protruding belly.

Would he recognize Chris?

Chris cleared his throat. The man looked around, and Chris saw his eyes widen just a fraction. Oh, yes, he knew who Chris was. Chris folded his arms.

"Can I help you, sir? Or would you like to keep shouting in my deputy's face?"

"You're the sheriff, are you?"

"Sheriff Foster."

Chris noted the skeptical way he was looked up and down at.

"You don't look old enough to be sheriff."

"Age has nothing to do with it, Mister...?"

"Yves Bracey." He drew himself up to his full height, merely an inch shorter than Chris. "I'm looking for my bride, Annie. She's missing."

Annie. Even Chris was trying not to cringe. He had teased Anne by calling her that before, but Anne had told him to stop. It upset her. So, Chris respected her wishes. Now he knew why she hated it.

"Your bride is missing. When did she go missing?"

"About six months ago. Suddenly vanished into the night with her little girl."

"She disappeared six months ago with her daughter."

Bracey groaned. "That's right, is everyone out here slow? That's what I said!"

"I heard what you said, and I'm just trying to understand." Chris barely reacted as Bracey growled at him. "It's been six months since she left. Either she's dead, or she disappeared for a reason. The fact you haven't been able to find her should have given you an indication that it was the latter."

"But we were going to get married! She was marrying me the day after she vanished. She knew this!" Bracey sighed and shook his head. "She was so eager for it, so the fact she left didn't sit right with me. Someone had to have kidnapped her."

"And you never received a note?"

"Nothing. We had almost given up hope. Then I hear that she might be down here." Bracey rubbed a hand over his chest. "A friend of mine said he had gone looking for his daughter, and he saw someone who looked like Annie. I knew it had to be her, especially when he described her little girl."

Chris bit back a snarl. Growcott. Somehow, he had managed to let Bracey know. Bracey had to have come down here on the fast coach to get into town when he did. Growcott had already almost gutted Chris, and now he had put Anne in danger. That man was more trouble than he was worth.

"And you didn't mind taking on a child that wasn't yours?"

"Tamsin's my niece. My brother died last year and made me promise to look after them. Annie and I..." A misty-eyed expression passed across his face. "We just fell in love. You have no idea how it feels to wake up and realize that the woman you love is gone."

Chris did know. More than he cared to admit. But he had learned how to read people a long time ago. Bracey was lying. He was putting on a very good performance, but there was no genuine emotion behind his words. Anyone else might have been taken in by him, but not Chris. Even if Anne hadn't just told him what was happening, there was no way he would let Bracey anywhere near her.

"If she left you, there's probably a good reason, Mr. Bracey."

"No! Annie had to have been kidnapped." Bracey looked a little put out that Chris wasn't immediately jumping to attention and doing his bidding. "She had some awful friends, and they would have spirited her away on some lies. I was too liberal with who was in her life, I should have put my foot down. That's my fault and I regret it."

From what Chris could tell, Yves Bracey regretted

not locking Anne in a room and throwing away the key.

"And you believe she's in Jefferson City?"

"Yes, I do. I've heard that she's here, and I want to bring her home. Or get married here." Bracey made a general gesture around him. "Doesn't look too bad here. I want to make her my wife as soon as possible. I've waited long enough."

Chris saw Terence was looking a little uncomfortable. No surprise, seeing as he had just escorted Anne into Chris' office. But he didn't say anything, letting Chris take charge. And Chris wasn't about to let this man near Anne if he could help it.

"Well, we can ask around..."

"I've already asked around! Nobody will tell me anything!"

That was something. Jefferson City townspeople were known to gossip, but they were also known to be very wary of people they didn't recognize, so they knew when to keep quiet. And after what had happened with Amy a couple of weeks back, everyone was incredibly uncomfortable with someone they didn't know. At least Growcott had done something right.

"If we hear anything about your bride, we'll let you know. We can't persuade her to return to you if she's a grown woman, but we can let you know that she's safe."

"Is that all?" Bracey scowled. "You can't do more than that?"

"She's not a criminal, and if there's a reason for her running, I'm not about to frighten her. If she is here, I'll make sure she's safe and well and let her decide." Chris spread his hands. "That's the best I can do."

Bracey snorted.

"I suppose that will have to do. Seeing as you've got nothing better to do. And don't lie to me."

"Would I have any reason to lie to you, Mr. Bracey?"

"Do you?"

Chris didn't blink, silently hoping that his face wasn't giving anything away. Bracey stared at him for so long Chris was sure he was going to cave in. Finally, the man huffed and turned away.

"Fine. I suppose I'll have to go with that. I'll be at the Jefferson Hotel when you need to get hold of me."

"I'll remember that."

Bracey strode out, banging the door closed behind him. Chris let out a sigh of relief. Terence's shoulders slumped.

"Sorry, Sheriff, I didn't know if I was supposed to say..."

"You did the right thing, Terence. And thanks for not directing him towards my office."

"Seeing as you had... Mrs. Bracey in there..." Terence's cheeks flushed. "I decided it was best to keep him here."

Chris grunted and turned away.

"If he comes back, just tell him we haven't found any sign of his bride yet and we'll come to him."

Chis was more worried than he let on. He knew Bracey hadn't been fooled. They both knew he knew Anne and that spelled trouble. Would that man go back to searching the town or would he come after Chris? It didn't matter, he would keep Anne safe no matter what.

He hurried into his office, where he found Anne still in her chair. She was hunched over and seemed to be rocking. Chris closed the door and knelt beside her chair, resting a hand on her back.

"Anne?"

Anne flinched, but she didn't move away. She had been crying, her white face streaked with tears. Chris's chest tightened at the sight. He reached out and brushed her tears away.

"He's not coming in. He's gone."

"You're not going to turn me over to him, are you?"

Chris stared. "You really think I would do that?"

"I know you won't, but..." Anne licked her lips. "I'm scared."

"I get that." Chris cupped her head, making her look at him. "And I'm not going to let him hurt you. I promise." And he intended to keep that promise no matter what.

CHAPTER FIVE

$\mathcal{A}$nne hadn't had an attack where she could barely breathe for months, but just the mere sound of Yves' voice had her freezing up and panicking. She had hoped to get away from him, that last night was just a fluke. But it wasn't. That had been Yves, and he was here.

She didn't want to go back there. She didn't want to be around Yves. He seemed to have the belief that he had first rights to Anne after his brother. Anne just wanted to get away from him. Why couldn't people accept what she wanted?

Jefferson City was a big change for her. People were kind, they didn't treat her harshly. There was an occasional person who thought they could speak to her in a way that had Anne wanting to cry, but there were always people to back her up. She hadn't had this many people looking out for her in a long time.

For the last few months, she had been feeling better about herself. She could do with putting weight back on, but she was focused on Tamsin and looking over her shoulder. It just took the slightest thing that reminded her of her in-laws and Anne was skittish. She couldn't do it forever, but she could make sure she didn't go back.

If Yves tried to kidnap her, Anne would fight. She would fight the whole way. Or run again. Someone would be able to hide her. Yves was a brute, and he was mean, but Anne could outrun him. If needed, she would get a gun. Anything to protect herself and Tamsin. If they went back, it wouldn't be to a wedding. It would more likely be to a coffin. And then who would look after Tamsin? Anne would not let that happen.

At least Chris hadn't given her away. The man had been steadfast for her over the recent months. Anne didn't know what she did to deserve it, especially when Chris had been so determined to keep her at arms length right from the beginning, but she was glad. Chris was certainly worth his weight in gold, even if he didn't believe it.

Just the feel of his arms around her made Anne feel better. She hadn't had anyone hold her with such gentleness since before Francois died. Anne had been reluctant to take embraces from her friends, and they understood that. With Chris, it seemed almost natural to allow him to hug her. He was softer and more gentle than he made himself out to be. And he was hurting, which had Anne wanting to soothe that for him. She wanted to look after him if he allowed it. When he was stabbed, Chris had allowed her to nurse him, even if he barely stayed in bed and wanted to get up and move around. He was stubborn, a typical Foster trait. Anne had to admire that about him, even if she wanted to smack him upside the head for being a fool with his health at times.

She wanted to go back to the boarding house, but Anne was afraid if she left Chris's office that Yves would see her and follow her back. She didn't want him to go back to Tamsin or put Tracy in danger. Tracy would fight for Tamsin, but Yves could easily push her aside. Anne wasn't about to drag anyone else into this.

So, Chris took her out the back of the station, across the yard, and into the house behind. His house. Anne stared as Chris pushed open the door.

"Why your house? Won't people see us?"

"Not here, it's very isolated considering where we are." Chris took off his Stetson. "And it's probably the last place he'd look. I'd like to think he believes the sheriff wouldn't lie to him, especially seeing as he knows I'm not afraid to use my gun."

"I wish you'd hit him," Anne muttered and grinned a little. She dithered on the threshold. "But I can't stay here, I…"

"I'm not suggesting you move in, Anne. Just until darkness comes and then I'll take you back to Maria's." Chris glanced over her shoulder. "If your brother-in-law is going around looking for you, then he's going to the obvious places."

Which included Maria's boarding house. Where Tamsin was. Anne felt the panic beginning to build.

"What about Tamsin?"

Chris sighed and took her arm, gently tugging her

into the house. He shut the door behind them, at which time Anne realized they were standing in his front room. It wasn't much, just simple. Nothing too fancy at all. For someone who came from a relatively wealthy family, Chris lived well within his means. No one would think he was a member of the Foster family just by looking at his home. But it was nice. Anne liked it. She had always preferred simplistic things in life. So had Francois.

A wash of sadness went over her. She missed him. He would be appalled at the way his family was treating his wife and child, and if he knew what Yves was planning Francois would have hightailed it out of town with Anne and Tamsin. They would never have to see his family again.

Anne watched as Chris crossed the room, tossing his Stetson onto the armchair by the unmade fire. Francois would have approved of him. He always said if he wasn't around, then he would want someone strong and dependable to look after his family. Anne had scolded him for talking that way, but Francois had stood by what he told her. Three days later, he was dead. And he would have been happy with Chris looking out for his wife.

If Francois hadn't died, I wouldn't be in this mess.

But then you wouldn't have met Chris.

"Don't you worry about Tamsin." Chris rubbed a hand over his face and gave her a gentle smile. "Terence will get the message to Tracy that Bracey is around, and he'll make provisions for Tamsin to head up to my brother's place. She'll be safe there."

"Will she be all right with James?"

"Of course. It's out of the way, so there's pretty much only one main road up from Jefferson City." Chris ran his fingers through his hair. "James has been a little over-protective since Amy's father tried to take her back, so he's not going to let anyone near Tamsin."

At least that was something. Anne had seen how James was around Amy, and she could believe that of James. After what happened, she couldn't blame him.

"He's fallen head over heels for Amy, hasn't he?"

"He has. So have my other brothers." Chris gave a dry chuckle. "Madmen that they are."

"Oh?" Anne folded her arms. "What's wrong with falling in love?"

"It's overrated."

He didn't look at her as he said it. Anne snorted.

"You said that six months ago, and you sounded believable then."

"You know what happened to me last Christmas." Chris sneered. "I'm sure it's the talk of the town."

Anne did know, but only because she had a lot of people talking about it when she was in earshot. She never addressed the rumors herself, choosing to stay out of it. Mostly because they seemed to change and get more outlandish each time things were said. However, if the rumors were anything to go by, she could understand why Chris was leery of Christmas and of getting married.

She moved to sit on the couch, smoothing down her skirts.

"I tend to prefer the source. The real events. And I respect the fact that you don't want to talk about it."

"What?" Chris stared at her. "You really don't know?"

"I know bits and pieces, but I don't know why. And it does change each time it reaches my ears." Anne shrugged. "I decided it was better to hear it from you if and when you were ready to talk. I'm not going to force you to tell me, as it's your choice."

Chris was staring at her as if he had never seen her before. Anne had to resist the urge to squirm. She had prided herself in not being confrontational unless she had to, and she didn't like to take things at face value. Chris Foster was a private man, as was she, and she respected that. It was up to him if he wanted to say anything.

"Your husband was a very lucky man to have someone like you," Chris murmured.

"I was lucky to have him."

Chris grunted. Then he sat on the couch beside her, resting his elbows on his knees, head bowed. Anne didn't move. She simply waited. It felt like a long time before Chris spoke, which almost made her jump.

"Olivia was my bride. She was... well, at the time I thought she was my everything. I adored her. Worshipped the ground she walked on. Then at the start of December, her childhood sweetheart came back. And Olivia started to change. It was subtle, but I noticed it. And I didn't like the fact that she was hanging around with her first love. I understand feelings might still be there, but it wasn't like that. It was... different. But Olivia always assured me that she was marrying me and he wouldn't come between us. Then it was Christmas Day and our wedding..."

He broke off. Anne knew this part, and it always left an ache in her heart knowing Chris had gone through that. Man or woman, that was not fair.

"She wasn't there."

Chris swallowed hard. He nodded.

"That was the most humiliating thing I've ever experienced. Standing there for nearly an hour before her father came in to tell me that Olivia had gone and she wasn't coming back. To hear who she had run off with..." He buried his head in his hands. "My brothers got me into a quiet room before I broke down. I've never done that since I became an adult except when Mother died. I didn't know what to do. I hated Christmas already, but that…"

"I know." Anne reached out and touched his back. He didn't pull away. "Why did you get married at Christmas if you hate it?"

"Because Olivia loved Christmas and I loved Olivia." Chris lowered his hands. "Now she's gone and I'm alone."

"You're not alone."

Chris snorted.

"Try telling that to this." He rubbed at his chest as he sat back, staring up at the ceiling. "I feel alone, even with my brothers around. I'm the youngest, so they treat me like a child at times. And I'm the sheriff! I should have some authority, even with my family. And I feel like I have the least."

He was lowering his guard. Anne could tell. Chris really did believe he was lonely. Shifting around to face him, Anne took a chance and reached out to stroke his head. Chris didn't pull away. If anything, he let out a sigh.

"Your brothers love you, Chris. And they do respect

you. I've seen it. Especially with Morgan. He's more protective of you than you realize. It's because you're the youngest that they want to look out for you. They tease you, but that's part of being a family. Those five have so much respect for you, and it's clear to see. But you know what men are like. Showing feelings makes them weak."

"You got that right."

Chris's eyes were closing, and he was leaning into Anne's touch. Anne smoothed a thumb over his forehead. Then she cupped his cheek and brushed her lips over his, which had Chris opening his eyes immediately.

"They love you and don't you ever doubt that. After what's happened in the last two weeks, I think they're allowed to look out for you like that. You've got family, more than I have right now. Don't push them away because they treat you as the baby brother." She stroked his cheek. "All right?"

Chris didn't immediately respond. He was staring at her. Then he reached up and brushed his fingers over her jaw, his hand sliding into her hair. Anne felt him tugging her head down and she didn't fight as his mouth touched hers.

His kiss was tentative, almost as if he was afraid she would pull away. Anne sighed and shifted closer, trying to deepen the kiss. She didn't want to pull away just yet. But Chris did, almost knocking her away as he broke the kiss and got to his feet, almost putting himself on the other side of the room.

"I'm sorry, Anne."

"Sorry?" Anne sat up. "What are you sorry for?"

"I..." Chris looked away. "I shouldn't have done that."

Anne snorted. He was ashamed for kissing her? That was not happening now. With a surge of courage Anne didn't know she possessed, she got to her feet.

"Do you see me complaining? And I kissed you first." She crossed the room and fisted her hands into his shirt, giving him a little shake. "Don't you dare start backing away now when I'm finally opening up to someone. Do you realize how hard it was to do that? I don't go around kissing people."

"I know you don't, and I'm sorry you felt that." Chris

hesitated and looked away. "I guess… I don't want to mess things up again."

"Chris." Anne cupped his jaw. "You didn't mess up. That's on your former bride, not you. And nothing is going wrong, other than your fear of being rejected again. I'm not going to reject you, believe me on that."

If anyone rejected Chris, they had to be mad. Rejecting any of the Foster brothers should have required you were looked at by a doctor. They were stubborn and could make a woman pull their hair out in frustration, but they were loyal, respectful, decent people. Olivia had walked away from a good man, and she didn't even care who she hurt in the process. And she still had a hold over Chris. Anne wanted to get rid of that hold.

Chris didn't speak for a moment, leaning into her hand. Anne brushed her thumb over his lips, and he turned to kiss her palm.

"Ernest has been telling me to go home and rest. I can get the deputies to sort out their duties while I'm recovering. Then I'll be home."

"All right." Anne gave him a smile. "I'll be here when

you get back. You were the one who brought me here. I'm not going anywhere."

Chris's shoulders slumped. He rested his forehead against hers for a moment before kissing her.

"Thank you." He stepped away and headed towards the door. "Make yourself at home. I won't be long."

Picking up his Stetson, Chris gave her one last glance before opening the door. He headed out into the cooling morning air, and then Anne was left feeling colder. She shivered and rubbed her arms. With a shiver, she determined to warm the place up before he got back.

After a quick hunt around in the house, Anne found some chopped firewood out the back. She brought some in and laid the fire. It didn't take much to get it lit, and then she settled onto the couch to watch the flames. She had loved doing that as a little girl, just staring into the fire to see it dance. It ended up being very hypnotic, something that was calming as a child.

It was certainly working now. Anne was feeling very tired. Although, that could be because she hadn't slept much the night before. Her head was still hurting, and her body ached from being thrown around like a rag doll. Perhaps she should close her eyes, rest herself for a bit. Chris wouldn't be back for a while, and Yves didn't know where she was. It could work.

Just for a little bit...

CHAPTER SIX

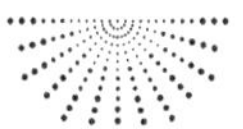

It didn't take long to sort out his deputies with their duties. Chris was glad when it was done because his stomach was starting to hurt again. Ernest had warned him if he did too much moving he would end up busting the stitches and making the wound even worse. Hoping he hadn't done too much damage, for once, Chris was happy to delegate the job to someone else. There had to be some perks to being the sheriff.

Some of his deputies were giving him knowing looks. It was like they knew he had kissed Anne. Chris ignored them. He was keeping someone safe, and he was going to rest. It wasn't their business beyond that.

Although the thought of going back and kissing Anne again did sound tempting. She really did taste as sweet as she looked.

When he finally got back to his house, the fire was burning nicely, warming up the room. Anne was fast asleep on the couch, one arm tucked underneath her. Chris stood over her and watched her sleep, her braid draped over her neck. She looked so relaxed like this, the lines of worry gone. She was far too young to be frowning so much, too young to be scared of someone coming after her.

I'm going to make sure that no one ever makes her scared again.

Gathering a blanket from the back of the couch, Chris draped it over her, brushing a hand over her hair. Then he settled on the couch opposite and stretched his legs out. It was certainly much warmer than before with the fire going. All too quickly, Chris found himself getting drowsy. A few moments with his eyes closed should make him feel a little better. Then he would see about finding alternative accommodations for Anne until Bracey was gone. Although, Chris was sure that Bracey wouldn't leave it at just that. The man was going to try to find her.

It was just ridiculous how people behaved, thinking they were entitled to anything they wanted, including their brother's wives. Chris had no time for them. Maybe it was because his father was like that.

Don't think about your father or you'll end up in a bad mood again. Focus on Anne.

In a moment. Once I've closed my eyes...

Chris wasn't sure what woke him, but it had him sitting up abruptly. The fire was still burning brightly, and Anne was still asleep. Holding his breath, he listened for a moment, thinking that it was his imagination playing up on him. But then he heard it again. A rattling sound. Someone was trying the back door.

Chris slid off his chair and scrambled over to the other couch. He shook Anne's shoulder hard enough that she jolted awake.

"Wh... what?" Anne's eyes were still glazed over as she opened them. "What is it?"

Chris put a finger to his lips and spoke in a whisper.

"Someone's trying the back door."

It took a moment for Anne to comprehend what was going on. Her eyes widened and she started to sit up.

"Oh, my!"

"Quiet!" Chris grabbed her arm, stopping her from falling off the couch. "Go out the front. Get my deputies. Tell them I need backup."

"All right." Anne started to get up, only to stare at him. "You're not coming?"

Chris pushed himself to his feet and withdrew his gun.

"I'm going to make sure he doesn't get near you."

"No!" Anne jumped to her feet. "He'll kill you."

"You underestimate me." Chris cupped her chin and pressed a hard kiss to her mouth. "Now stop arguing and go!"

This time, Anne didn't argue with him. She hurried towards the door and was out with a final glance back at him. Chris heaved a sigh of relief. At least she wasn't going to get hurt once Bracey got into the house. It had to be him; seeing as everyone in town knew who lived here, he was the only one stupid enough to break into the sheriff's home.

Chris headed into the kitchen, just as the back door broke inwards and Bracey came through. He was holding a gun in his hand, which was aimed at Chris's chest. Chris aimed his at Bracey's head.

"Put your gun down and your hands on your head, Bracey. You're breaking and entering into the sheriff's home."

"Not going to happen." Bracey sneered. "The only person who's putting their gun down is you."

Chris braced himself, ready for gunfire. But nothing happened. Bracey was still pointing his weapon at him, but he didn't pull the trigger. Anne had called her in-laws brawlers. In Chris's mind that translated to cowardice. Bracey may have a gun and liked using his weight to get what he wanted, but he wouldn't be able to pull the trigger. He wasn't brave enough for that.

Don't underestimate him or you might end up coming out in a coffin.

"Where is she, Foster?"

"Where's who?"

Bracey snarled.

"Don't play games with me. You said you didn't know who Annie was. Then I'm told that she's often in your company!"

"Who said that to you?"

"Someone in the general store told me." Bracey gestured at the gun. "Once I gave him a bit of persuasion, that is."

Chris bit back the snarl. He had threatened civilians. Even if he hadn't broken in, Bracey was going to jail. He just had to get the gun away from the man before it went off.

"Anne Bracey is not your bride. She's your brother's widow. And she wanted to come here. What she does with her life is her business, not yours."

"She promised herself to me!" Bracey shouted. "Francois said she was mine once he was gone!"

"I highly doubt that Anne's husband would have passed her around the family."

Bracey sniggered.

"You don't know our family. We keep things to ourselves. Now, where's Annie, Foster?"

He advanced on Chris, but Chris didn't waver. It was only when Bracey was about to be prodded in the face with Chris' pistol that he stopped. Chris was taller, but Bracey had the weight and he wasn't recovering from life-threatening injuries. He could take Chris if he so wanted. Chris could only hope he had a few bits of common sense left to back off.

"You're not taking her back. She doesn't want to go."

"You think you're going to stop me? You look like you're about to keel over."

"I am the sheriff."

"You're younger than I am!" Bracey scoffed. "You think I'm going to listen to a mere child?"

"I also happen to be the son of the mayor here." Chris saw a slight flicker in the other man's eyes. Was he worried about that? Good. "He can be a pain in the backside, but he's fiercely protective of his children."

There was a slight movement behind Bracey, and Chris caught sight of Adam in the doorway. When had he turned up? But that did make Chris feel better knowing one of his brothers was close by.

Bracey drew himself up to his full height and squared his shoulders.

"My father is friends with the governor," he said smugly.

"You trump me, fine. But that doesn't mean you get to kidnap Anne and her daughter from a life they wanted."

"You can keep the brat. I just want Annie."

Chris stared. "You'd throw your niece away?"

"She's not my child." Bracey shrugged. "And she was a pest to my parents. Who wants her after that?"

Chris felt sick at that comment. "You're disgusting."

"Am I?" Bracey looked Chris up and down, still looking smug. "At least I've got a woman. What do you have? Nothing. Not since your girl left you at the altar. What does that say about you?"

Chris didn't respond. He wasn't going to let Bracey have that. There was a sound behind him and then

Bracey was pointing his gun at Chris's head, the barrel inches from Chris's nose.

"Stay where you are! I'll shoot if you move!"

"Can't do that." Chris almost sagged in relief when he heard Matt's voice. "You're in my brother's house. And if you kill the sheriff, you'll be lynched before you ever see the inside of a courtroom."

From the way the gun was trembling in Bracey's hand, he knew it. Adam moved into the kitchen and Bracey almost hit Chris in the head as he spun around to point his gun at Adam.

"Let me guess. Another brother."

"Sure is." Adam folded his arms, leaning against the counter. "There's three more of us if you'd like to draw this out."

"So you would gang up on one man?"

"Why not? You attack young women in alleyways and threaten a lawman while trying to kidnap her." Matt leaned on the doorframe.

Chris could see him out of the corner of his eye. His hand was on his holster. "You threaten one of us, you threaten all of us. Especially with our little brother. And you're not having Anne."

As he spoke, Morgan appeared in the kitchen doorway. He stepped over the broken door and moved into the room. Chris caught his eye, and Morgan gave him a slight head nod.

Bracey scoffed. He was still focused on Matt.

"You're going to make me go away? I don't think you can take me on in a fight." He spun the gun around his finger, fumbling a little. "I've got a gun."

"Who said this was going to be a fight?"

"I did." Bracey smirked. "I'm older, stronger, and I wasn't stabbed in the gut. I can take your brother on." He gestured at Chris. "And I can take both of you on, easy. Just one bullet, and..."

"Really?" Matt arched an eyebrow. "If you're going to shoot us, why haven't you done so already?"

Bracey's smirk faded a little. Chris glanced at Morgan, who moved a little closer. He was now standing practically behind Bracey. It was a wonder the man hadn't even noticed him. Chris's arm was getting tired. He lowered his gun, keeping it pointed at Bracey's stomach.

"What do you know about my family, Bracey? Seeing as you know about what happened to me, do you know about my brothers?"

"What's that got to do with this?"

"Morgan is the eldest. And he's a US Marshal. You kidnap Anne, you're going to have to run fast because he'll be after you."

Bracey looked a little bewildered. Surely, he did know? If you mentioned one Foster in Jefferson City, the others always got mentioned. It was common knowledge. Bracey recovered himself quickly and sneered.

"Threatening me with that isn't going to scare me."

"Are you sure about that?" Chris glanced at Morgan. "He's pretty big."

As it was, Morgan was so close to Bracey he was almost pressed up against his back. It was quite amusing. Adam looked like he was trying not to laugh, and Chris was trying to fight back a smile. Bracey rolled his eyes.

"Don't bother scaring me like that. If he's big, then I'll just gut him like I'm going to gut you. No one's keeping me away from Annie."

Chris glanced at Matthew, who looked slightly bemused. He turned back to Bracey.

"Let me get this straight. You just threatened two lawmen in front of witnesses?"

"I didn't threaten." Bracey lifted his head up. "I made a promise."

"Want to keep that promise?" Morgan growled in his ear.

Bracey cried out and turned around, bumping off Morgan's chest. He stumbled back towards Chris. Chris rammed the butt of his gun into Bracey's head, which had Bracey dropping like a stone. He almost took Chris down with him before Chris darted out of the way. Bracey hit the ground hard, the gun skittering away across the floor. His eyes rolled up into his head and closed. Then he didn't move.

Chris knelt down and took the gun away before checking the man was still alive. He was, his heartbeat still pumping. Chris looked up at Morgan.

"Why didn't you hit him?"

"He came in and threatened you." Morgan shrugged and gave him a lopsided smile. "You get the first whack."

Chris had to roll his eyes at that. He tried to get up and winced as his stomach screamed at him. Hitting the man was going to be a little too much movement.

"Chris?" Matt was there, taking his arm and helping him to his feet. "Take it easy. I've got you."

"Thanks." Chris couldn't stop himself from leaning against his brother. It felt good to do that for the first time in years. "I think I need to sit down."

"Then sit." Morgan took Bracey's gun and put it on the table. "Adam and I have got this fool. You focus on you."

Chris wasn't about to argue with that.

CHAPTER SEVEN

Anne's heart was racing as she paced around Chris's office. Matthew Foster had come into the station looking for his brother when Anne came in to tell the deputies what happened. Matthew had taken charge, dispatching the deputies and then telling Anne to stay in the office until they had dealt with Yves.

Anne wasn't about to argue with that. She would happily never see Yves again. Or any of his family. They could go to hell, as far as she was concerned, and leave her and Tamsin in peace.

She could only hope that Chris was all right. He couldn't take Yves on in a physical fight, not with the way he was. Yves could overpower him, and then he would come after Anne. But the thought of Chris getting hurt was causing a pain in her chest. Maybe she shouldn't have left him?

He won't. Chris will deal with him. He's going to be fine.

Worry had Anne pacing around the room, unable to sit down.

When the door finally opened, Anne was almost beside herself with worry. She had heard a lot of shouting and cursing, most of it coming from Yves. But Anne didn't dare step foot outside the office; she didn't want to see Yves. That would likely set him off again. However, it did sound like Chris and Matthew had things under control.

Anne's heart didn't stop racing until the door opened and Chris came in. He looked pale, and his hand was pressing at his stomach, but he was walking.

"Chris…"

He was all right. Upright, at least. Anne found herself bursting into tears.

"Anne?" Chris closed the door and crossed the room,

wrapping his free arm around her. "What is it? There's no need to cry."

"I'm sorry, I... I was so scared." Anne leaned her head on his shoulder. "I thought... I thought he..."

"Well, he didn't." Chris rocked her gently. "I had a little backup. My brothers certainly know when to make an entrance."

Anne looked up.

"I thought it was just Matt."

"Adam and Morgan turned up as well. Ernest was coming into the station as we put Bracey into the cells. The man's going to have a nasty headache for a while, so we did need a doctor." Chris rolled his eyes. "Ernest would rather have the man suffer, but his conscience kicked him moments after he said it."

Anne could very well believe that. She placed a hand over his as it rested on his belly.

"He didn't hurt you, did he?"

"No. I've just had a little too much movement. I need to sit down."

Anne tugged him over to the chair and made him sit

down. Chris did so, rather heavily with a relieved sigh. Anne knelt before him.

"So, you got Yves?"

"We did. Morgan's going to send word for a colleague of his to take Bracey back to where he came from, with instructions that he and his family are not permitted in Jefferson City for fear of arrest." Chris chuckled. "From what Morgan said, his colleagues will likely want to stay home for Christmas, so Bracey is going to have to stay in the cells until after the festivities are over unless he's really lucky."

"Morgan's not going to take him?"

"He's getting married soon. He doesn't want to be away on his wedding day. And you live quite a way away, don't you?"

"I guess." Anne blinked. "Wait, he's getting married soon? That's quick."

"Weddings happen fast over here." Chris took off his Stetson and placed it on the couch beside him. "He and my brothers are mad. The four of them have decided to get married on Christmas Day."

Anne stared. That she had not been expecting, especially when they all knew what Mayor Foster was trying to do before.

"I thought you all agreed that wouldn't happen."

"This isn't for Father. This is for us." Chris rubbed a hand over his face. He looked exhausted. "He's not taking that away from us."

At least they were realizing that they weren't going to let their father think he was in charge. They were behaving like grown men for once. Anne squeezed his knees.

"I'm glad you're all right. Well, within reason. I was scared when I realized Yves was trying to get in."

Chris's expression softened. He reached out and cupped her cheek in his hand.

"I'm fine. He wasn't going to get one over on me. That's happened twice in as many weeks." He smiled. "I'm not going to let it happen again."

Anne certainly hoped not. She didn't want to have to worry about Chris being reckless anymore. If she had a choice, she would tell him to find something a little less dangerous as a job. But that would mean taking away what Chris was. And Anne didn't want to do that. Chris wouldn't be the same man, and she preferred the man she knew. Certainly when he was more amenable.

Rising up, Anne grabbed his head and kissed him. Chris started, but he didn't pull away this time. This time, he pulled her closer and kissed her back. When they finally came up for air, Chris looked a little bewildered.

"What was that for?"

"It was either that or throttle you." Anne eased back and swatted his shoulder. "You took him on? Yves could've killed you."

"He was a coward. He would never have pulled the trigger."

Anne gasped. "He had a gun? Chris!"

"He didn't use it on me." Chris held up a hand as Anne started to protest. "As I said, the man's a coward. Besides, Yves wasn't about to win when my brothers were there to back me up."

He was so sure about that. Anne shook his head.

"Your family is mad."

"I know. But they do it for people they love." Chris shrugged. "It's a redeeming feature, according to Tracy."

"Sounds about right." Then Anne noticed that Chris was looking at her intently. "What?"

"I don't think you heard me correctly, Anne. They do it for people they love. So do I." Chris took her hand and kissed it. "It's why I stood up to Yves as I did."

"What are you saying, Chris?"

Chris stared and looked away.

"You're going to make me say it, aren't you? I haven't said those words to a woman since Olivia left. It's not easy." He took a deep breath and looked back at her. "The fact that I... well, it scared me. I knew I should keep my distance but... I couldn't. I just couldn't walk away."

Anne didn't need him to say he loved her. Just seeing the look in his eyes told her everything. It would take time for him to say those words out loud, but Anne didn't care. She cupped his jaw, feeling the rough bristles under her palm.

"And I couldn't walk away, either. I told myself that I should, and I couldn't."

"Really?"

"Really." Anne kissed him. "Just so you know, Tamsin comes with me. You get both of us."

"I know that, and I wouldn't expect anything less." Chris shifted her off the floor and onto his lap, allowing her to curl against his chest as he sat back. "And I have no objections. I adore her. Just like I adore her mother."

Anne smiled. That was the closest she was going to get. She would take it.

"You're good at softening me up."

"I hope so because I'm not into flowery conversation." Chris kissed her head. "I prefer straightforward talking."

"So do I. Although, I hope you do know how I'm feeling about you."

"I do." Chris's arms tightened around her. "It's going to take time for us to open up, but I know I can do it.

And I know you can, too." He kissed her head. "I don't want you going anywhere, Anne."

"I wasn't planning to. But if you want me to stay properly..."

"Marry me." It wasn't a question. Chris smiled as he cupped Anne's head, brushing his lips over hers. "I think we both deserve a second chance... I love you. Marry me."

"Isn't that supposed to be a question?" she asked but there was a smile in her voice. His mouth opened and closed but she stopped his protests by kissing him.

"Yes, I'll marry you but I thought you couldn't say it just yet."

"Sometimes the heart has a way of surprising you."

She kissed him again. "Yes it does and I love you too"

Anne smiled as she rested her head on his shoulder.

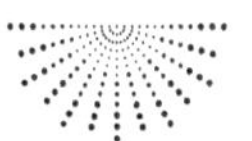

$\mathcal{A}$nne was so exhausted she had almost fallen asleep without getting undressed. Tracy managed to help her into her nightgown and got her friend into bed beside her sleeping daughter. Tamsin barely woke up and her mother simply curled up next to her. After what had been going on a few hours previously, Tracy couldn't blame her.

Yves had to have been mad to think he would get his own way like that. Then again, that family had always been entitled and believed they were right all the time. Francois was the only person who came out of that family with any sense of decency.

Tracy knew Francois would approve of Chris. He would have wanted Anne looked after, protected from his family. Chris had certainly done that. Anne couldn't have asked for better than him.

Thankfully, Tamsin was not going to know about any of this. Tracy, Polly, and Amy had spent all day distracting the little girl up at the ranch, Tamsin showing them how much she loved horses. It didn't take much to have her so worn out she was falling asleep on the way back once they had word Yves had been arrested. She didn't deserve to be caught in the middle of this.

Fingers crossed, Yves would leave Anne alone. Chris and his brothers would make sure he didn't set eyes on Anne again. Tracy was certain of that.

She let herself out of her friend's room, closing the door quietly. A yawn stretched her jaw, she was worn out. She loved children, but they were hard work. Anne was stronger than she realized.

"Tracy?"

Tracy gasped and spun around. Her heart picked up speed when she saw Thomas Brooks stepping out of Shelley's room just down the hall. Tracy pressed a hand to her chest, wishing that she didn't feel so lightheaded when the pastor was around.

"Pastor Tom. I... I didn't realize you were here."

"I came to see Maria." Thomas nodded at Shelley's now closed door. "And to make sure Shelley was all right with baby Oliver."

"And is she?"

"Absolutely fine."

Thomas walked over to her, barely making a sound with his footsteps. He was a very tall man, a very muscular one, and yet he was the most light-footed man Tracy had ever met. A shiver washed over her as he approached her. His sheer size made Tracy feel positively tiny when she stood next to him. Tiny but safe. Very safe.

Falling for the pastor wasn't exactly what she had in mind when she arrived in Jefferson City, and Tracy was still struggling with it. She considered herself a confident woman, but not as far as Thomas Brooks was concerned.

"How's Tamsin?" Thomas asked.

It took Tracy a moment to realize what he had just said. Clearing her throat, she drew herself up to her full height.

"She's asleep now. So is Anne. Even exhausted as she was, Anne looked happier than I've seen her in a while."

"After what happened, I'm not surprised. Yves Bracey's antics are all over town now."

"That part I'm not surprised about." Tracy smoothed her hands down her skirts "Not many people, especially men, want to deal with that."

"The Foster brothers are different." Thomas gave a slight smile, his eyes warming. "They stand up for what is right and they stand by those they love. That was one of the reasons I agreed to bring you ladies here. I knew they were all good men and that no matter what happened you would all be cared for, even though they hated to show their good side at first."

Tracy wasn't about to argue with that. The six brothers had been stand-offish and prepared to dislike Tracy and her friends since they arrived. All of them knew what the events were that brought them together, and none of them liked it. But the girls had made the best of it, and now five out of the six brothers were going to be married. That just left

Ernest, but with his heart clearly set on Jacira, it wouldn't be long before he did the same as his brothers.

Tracy didn't mind that she wasn't one of the women chosen as a bride. She was happy that her friends found love, especially Polly. She and Morgan were definitely made for each other. But the longer things went on, the more Tracy felt a pang of regret it wouldn't happen for her. Not when she realized that she had fallen for someone else.

Six months of being in his company had been painful to handle. Tracy felt like she was punishing herself being with Thomas Brooks, but she couldn't help it. She wanted to be around him. And he allowed it with that easygoing smile of his and the twinkling of his beautiful eyes. He was just beautiful all over.

"You get some rest, Tracy." Thomas reached out and brushed a strand of hair over her ear. "You look worn out. You should feel better with some sleep."

"I... I expect so." Tracy was momentarily distracted by the touch of his fingers. She bit her lip and nodded. "I'll do... I'll do that. Goodnight, Thomas."

"Goodnight."

Tracy's room was only the next room over, and even then she struggled to open the door. She stumbled into her room, shutting the door behind her before she said something more stupid. Collapsing against the door, Tracy thumped her head on the solid wood. Oh, why did she sound so silly? Thomas had the ability to make her tongue-tied in the worst possible moments.

The attraction was certainly there on both sides, but Thomas was refusing to do anything about it. He kept himself emotionally distant when he thought he was getting a little close for comfort. But then Tracy remembered how the pastor had been when it was implied by Mayor Foster that he had his eye on Tracy. Thomas was furious about that. Jealous, even. Would that be enough?

Tracy didn't know, but she was certain about one thing; she was not going to become another Mrs. Foster.

We hope you enjoyed this story read on for a preview of the next brother's story. Will he find a wonderful new love or will danger and a fire take it all away before he can admit his feelings? Read on to find out.

Did you miss book 1, Nicola? Grab it here

Jacira smiled down at the three-week-old baby in her arms, now sleeping soundly. He was so beautiful. The little cute face warmed her heart for she adored children, especially newborns. They were just so tiny, so trusting. They weren't judgmental. None of them gave her strange looks or gave her a wide berth.

To be a child again. Before...

Jacira pushed that thought aside and turned to the mother of the baby, who was sitting on the couch looking like she hadn't slept for a week.

Jacira gave her a gentle smile and passed her little Zachariah.

"He'll be much better now, Mrs. Winstanley."

"Oh, thank you!" Carla Winstanley looked relieved as she took her son. "I felt like I was going mad with his crying. I didn't know what to do."

"It was just a lot of trapped wind in his belly. That can be uncomfortable." Jacira stroked Zachariah's head, which had him smiling in his sleep. "Just burp him a bit more after you've fed him, and it should be all right. And I suggest that you get some sleep while he does."

"I certainly will."

Carla looked eager at the thought of sleeping. Being a first-time mother was always difficult, and Jacira could sympathize with the time it took to get used to the new routine. She had never had children herself, but she saw the struggles of other women, how strong they had to be to make sure their children were fed and well cared for while remaining strong themselves. Jacira could only hope that would be her someday.

If you're lucky. Men aren't exactly forthcoming with their offers of courtship. Nobody wants to marry a scarred Indian woman.

"You're an absolute wonder, Jacira," Carla said. "You just seem to have a magic touch when it comes to children."

"I just know how to read a person." Jacira stepped back and began to gather her things. "Especially little mites who can't talk for themselves. Zachariah won't be able to tell you things for a while," she said with a smile, "but if you watch him, he will in his own way. You will soon start to see those signs."

"I bet it'll be like my husband's nephews when he does." Carla kissed Zachariah's head. "Once he starts, he won't be able to stop."

"All children are like that when they realize they can talk they like the sound of their own voice."

Carla made a face.

"Hopefully, Zachariah won't be like his nephews."

Jacira bit back what she really wanted to say. Carla's brother-in-law had three children over the age of five from his first wife and two under three from his second wife, and they were not the best behaved. They were allowed to run rampant and cause chaos. Their parents just didn't seem to discipline them.

Jacira took a lot of abuse from the older boys, and their father did nothing to stop it. It was like he was enjoying seeing her called horrible names.

The only thing she could do was ignore it. Even if it did make her want to cry. Stephen Winstanley didn't listen to anyone except himself.

"That's up to the parents." Jacira chose her words carefully. "How you and your husband raise him will factor into how he behaves. You raise him properly, then he'll be a good person."

Carla smiled. "That was a very subtle jab at my brother-in-law's parenting, wasn't it?"

"I'm not going to voice my opinions on people, Mrs. Winstanley. It's not my place to."

Carla laughed.

"You're so diplomatic, Jacira. Not like Doctor Foster at all. He certainly likes to voice his opinion."

"I certainly know about that."

After working with Ernest Foster for five years, Jacira knew how vocal he was about things, especially towards his brothers. Certainly in the last year when he and his brothers discovered their father had organized for women to come to Jefferson City to pair off with them in marriage. The brothers had vowed it would not happen, but now the other five brothers had fallen for the newcomers. All of them had decided to get married on or around Christmas Day.

When she had heard of this development, Jacira had been concerned. Ernest wasn't one to change his opinion, but the women were beautiful. She had thought one of them would catch Ernest's eyes. And yet it hadn't happened. Why did that make her feel a little better about her position?

Because you've been in love with him since you met. And you haven't said a word about it.

"How do you put up with him?" Carla asked.

"I beg your pardon?"

"Working with Ernest. You've been here for five years and you barely bat an eyelid at his reactions."

Jacira smiled.

"You get used to it. I've heard worse outbursts from lots of other people." That was not always fun.

"Besides, you know if Doctor Foster is doing it, then he is fair and it is because he cares too much. It's just the way he is."

"I've known him for twenty years and I'm still not used to it." Carla shrugged. "Then again, he was almost sixteen when I met him. He was loud and a little arrogant then."

"He can be loud, but you know his heart is in the right place." Jacira paused. "If there's something wrong or you're not in his good books, he'll let you know."

That had happened a couple of times when they had first met, but Jacira was a fast learner. She stood firm in her beliefs and opinions, but she knew when to pick her battles with Ernest. Even now, although he seemed to be a lot more amenable around her. Which, coming from Ernest, seemed a little strange.

Jacira could still remember the day she met Ernest. He was so tall that he could barely get through the doorway, his dark hair trimmed close to his collar with a trimmed beard. His eyes could twinkle when he was in a good mood, but when he was in a bad mood they were like black diamonds. Scary didn't begin to describe it. Ernest was one of those people who you would not think that he was a doctor at all, and yet he was the most efficient, gentle man Jacira knew.

She was jerked out of her thoughts when she heard a door open and shut very close by. She looked at the clock. At this time of the day, Daniel would be at the forge working. And it wasn't lunchtime, so why was he back so early?

Then Jacira heard a voice that had her heart sinking.

"Carla? Are you around?"

"I'm in here, Stephen," Carla called back. "The kitchen."

A large man filled the doorway, ducking his head to get through the door. Jacira found herself getting to her feet quickly so she didn't feel towered over. Which was not easy, seeing as Stephen was six-five of solid muscle. Ernest was the same height, and yet Jacira never felt intimidated by him… but Stephen Winstanley wore intimidation like a coat.

"Sorry about bothering you, Carla." Stephen

approached Carla and kissed her cheek. "I just bought something that Daniel said he needed…"

His voice trailed off when he saw Jacira. His relaxed expression hardened and Jacira saw his eyes turn into slits.

"Why is she here?"

"I asked Jacira here to help me with Zachariah." Carla glanced between her brother-in-law and Jacira. "He wouldn't settle."

"Really?" Stephen's scowl darkened. "We could've handled that ourselves."

Jacira took a deep breath and slowly counted to ten. Her heart was racing. It did this every time Stephen was anywhere near her. Ever since being shunned from her tribe and coming to Jefferson City, he was the only man who could make her feel genuine fear.

"She shouldn't be in here," Stephen went on with a growl. "We don't have her kind in our homes."

Carla gasped. "She's not going to hurt anyone, Stephen! She's a healer."

"Sounds like a cover to me," Stephen grunted. He

straightened to his full height. Even with space between them, he towered over Jacira. "Ugly Indians like her shouldn't be allowed in polite society."

Jacira's stomach twisted. She hated it when Stephen pointed out her obvious defects. That hadn't always been the way, but once he realized she wasn't going to give him the answer he wanted Stephen had turned on her. It had been sudden, and it still hurt even now. The words that came out of his mouth still made her hair stand on end.

"And you call what you're saying polite?" Carla shot back sharply. "I didn't ask for you to come in here to insult my guest, especially when they're helping me so much."

"We don't need a *healer* here." Stephen sneered at the word 'healer'. "If anything happens to Zachariah, we can handle it. Or get Doctor Foster."

Carla glowered at him and turned to Jacira with a look of sympathy.

"Ignore him, Jacira. He's not the patient here. I'm sure Zachariah will be happy to have you help him."

"I'm sure." Jacira managed a tiny smile as she picked

up her bag. "If you have any other problems with him, bring him to the surgery."

"To Doctor Foster," Stephen snapped. "Not this witch. Come on, you," he grabbed Jacira's arm and hauled her towards the door, "out."

Jacira stumbled but somehow managed to keep upright as Stephen dragged her out of the house. He pushed her forward as they stepped out onto the street, giving her a hard shove in her back. Jacira tripped and fell to her knees. She ignored the pain in her knees and the throbbing in her ankle as she stood up and swung around on him.

"I was helping with your nephew, Stephen!" she cried. "You don't need to treat me like that!"

"Maybe I do." Stephen folded his arms, his huge frame blocking the doorway. "Carla may trust you, but I don't. And neither does Daniel."

Jacira begged to differ on that, but she wasn't about to do it in the street. It was a busy day and people were already watching them after she had been catapulted from the house. She could feel her face burning from embarrassment as she glared at

Stephen, who looked like he was enjoying her discomfort.

"You can't block me from doing my job because you don't like where I come from. Or what I said to you. That's just childish."

"I will do more than that if you keep harassing my sister-in-law."

"It wasn't harassment!"

"From where I'm standing, it looks just like that." Stephen turned away, effectively dismissing her. "Don't step foot in my family's house again, or you'll live to regret it."

"You don't live there. You can't tell me what to do in someone else's house."

But Stephen didn't answer. He simply disappeared back inside, slamming the door behind him.

Jacira wiped at her eyes to prevent a tear and raised her head. The words hurt, they always did even though they were unjust. Turning away she put a smile on her face and noticed that most people were no longer staring. Why did some people have to be so cruel?

I hope you enjoyed this brief preview of Jacira in this much loved new series. If you are on our newsletter we will let you know as soon as the books are available, if not join here

In the meantime have you read our latest Christmas Box Set? Grab it here

To receive two free Mail Order Bride Romance join Fair Havens Books exclusive newsletter. http://eepurl.com/bHou5D

If you liked this book you would love:

Read now **Massive 40 Book Joint Box set of sweet inspirational romances.**

If you would like to find all of my books, look on my Amazon page

While there, click the yellow follow button for updates.

God bless,

Indiana Wake

www.ingramcontent.com/pod-product-compliance
Lightning Source LLC
Chambersburg PA
CBHW071530150726
48000CB00002B/739